Squaw Winter

By

Virginia Love Long

The Kindred Spirit
Rt. 2, Box 111
St. John, Kansas 67576

Some of the poems in this book were previously published as follows: "Centering" in WINDHOVER, N.C. State University; "Amazon Patrol" and "Constancy/Change" in CRUCIBLE, Atlantic Christian College; "Quena" and "Hymn to Coatlicue" in PEMBROKE MAGAZINE, Pembroke State University; "Divorce" in WRITERS' CHOICE, The Greensboro Group; "Missing In Action" and "Degrees of Light" in THE PILOT, Southern Pines; "Squaw Winter" and "This Is A Song Of Old Men" in UPSTREAM, a book by the author; and TALKING TO TOCI in THE FORUM FOR UNIVERSAL SPOKESMEN, Issue No. 2, Willow Bee Publishing House, and New KAURI. "14 Southern Cihuacuicatl" were chosen for Honorable Mention in International Poetry Review's Original English Contest in 1980 by William Meredith, consultant in poetry at the Library of Congress.

© 1987 by Virginia Love Long

    Art by Dawn Senior

Library of Congress Catalog
Number: 87-81715

ISBN: 0-943795-00-1

Second Printing, 1989

for my Mother

Preface

Squaw Winter is a time when there is deep snow, but the ground is not frozen underneath. No doubt, such a paradoxical phenomenon has something to do with lunation. This volume, which harkens back to Aztec lamentations and love songs, while echoing prayers and requests of more modern Native American tribes, is rich in the imagery and mystical symbolism of both nature and the moon. And yet, the poignant phases of woman seem to bloom and die in haunting lyricism that returns rhythm and the shimmering beauty of language to poetry wed to a contemporary narrative form.

There is a deep chanting magic in SQUAW WINTER that leads us to the painful piercing side of human belief that is vulnerable and therefore prone to myriad disappointments coupled with risks. But the Illuminations that result from such total embracing of life penetrate our own minds and urge us to alter or transform personal focus to experience these broader, more encompassing visions.

These poems unfold from a direct contact with earth, fire, wind, water: animals and trees; the sun and the moon; man and woman; and each of us ever and always alone with the knowledge and meaning evolved from exploring emotions, the most central and changing of which is Love.

Rochelle Lynn Holt
November 15, 1985

Centering

"The void is the creatrix, the matrix. It is not mere hollowness and anarchy. But in women it has been identified with lovelessness, barrenness, sterility. We have been urged to fill our 'emptiness' with children. We are not supposed to go down into the darkness of the core."
—Adrienne Rich

Going down to dark's heart,
I am amazed
At these spacious skies.
We are fractions,
Incomplete suns,
Unfinished wholes,
Whatever we dare to make
Of our unfinished selves.
Like the butterfly
Clinging tenaciously to the rose,
I touch down upon the motherlode
And stare while seeds of light
Shower flowering
Into stars.
I throw lightning,
Strike fire
Everywhere I go.

Constancy/Change

O the changes written across Love's countenance!
Reworked, rewrought, recast, rendering the heart
Stranger anew! Like the shivering barnswallows
Sweeping through the grey winter dawn, I pass
From nest to nest, huddle in the secret hollows
Of inhospitable water-oaks, dream each awakening
Into the arms of reality, and fly on, on, on,
Still alone. Love licks at my bones
And the ghosts of loves unknown
Drink honey from the well of my womb.
I dissolve, melting into homeless fog.
Hungry winds howl dirges at every door;
Broken half-notes dangle from each hand
Too heavy with flesh to catch love's full bloom.
I would rain love down like righteousness
Were I a full god, like Them,
They-Who-Guard-The-Gates-Of-Sky,
But I am woman and like the moon
Can only change, change, change.

Because Our Ways Are So Much One

I love too the narrow country roads, empty
Of sun's gold, the thin tears of rain
Staining the fogged glass. Already the winds
Have ransacked the shrinking camellias.
Red petals plaster mailboxes and sputtering dogs.
The lost petals are glued between my fingers,
Cold lips mouthing wet kisses behind my knees,
Mumbling to the drooping twigs of faded lilacs
You left behind to haunt the hushed room.
I have never heard so much silence.
You carry so much of life's goodness with you.
With you you carry so much of my brighter self,
I work the mirror's face, hoping to trace
A fragment of my own, to find
Only the tangled twigs and crimped petals
Strewn across yesterday's nest. Outside
The wind dogs prowl in the shadowy trees.
Small streams are spilling over the high pasture
And gray waters swamp the shallow lowland.
Rain claws at the rattling screen
And through the west window I see
The drooping bellies of dark clouds finally full term,
Straining sky's girdle, shaking thunder loose
To deliver the lost words:
                    Eros. Phileo. Agape.
The trinity of my waking heart unfolds
Its new season's offering like the young leaves
Shaking out their groping green spears
And I know that of all earthly paths
Love's way shines both first and best,
The road of love I will always choose to walk barefoot
And brazen as moon's silvery winding sheets
And when you cannot share the way
The winds walk with me, hand in hand.
They carry the echoes of your excited heart
And whispering, tremble every churchbell
To rising jubilation, ringing out victory hymns
To love unheard.

All The Lost Loves Come Home

The steel grey clouds gather like snowbirds
Sheltering in the anguished trees
Stripped leafless back to the bare bark
Naked to the north wind's sharp teeth.
The empty fields are laid by
Covered over with the blinding green
Of winter wheat. The last roses surrender
Their drooping petals in gusty flurries
Taken in by the waiting mounds
Of brittle leaves. The chill of the dim back porch
Is heavy with the fragrance of winesap apples
And sweet potatoes. Another summer has gone
And another harvest has come. The richness
Of life's growing bounty awes.
All the lost loves come home nesting
In my heart. My blood is strong
And I have the lion's heart: I fear neither
Living nor dying. I am another world,
A virgin stand of longleaf pines riddled
With secret groves of wild holly
And enchanted glades. I am a moon daughter
And mother of night. My loves are strong, too,
Wild as the woods are deep. I am summer
In your heart now, as well as my own.
I rock love by the stove like a baby
Safe against my heart. I call to you
In the growing nights: come home, come home,
Your love heartens, hones me. Love is
A country road we walk, wandering,
Weaving dreams, spinning new stars.

How Love's Seasons Spin

I had forgotten how Psyche had her tasks,
Like Hercules, assigned as divine testing,
And how quietly unremarked —
The unglorious sorting, sifting;
The learning to wait and allow destinies
To unfold themselves; then the gathering
Of golden fleeces, avoiding the rams
And collecting the harvest from the thorn groves;
Next the glass of water from the Styx River,
One goblet at a time; and finally going
Down to Persephone's house far underground,
Going down to Death's house, alone.
Just as she found herself on death's mountain,
I had forgotten how love's seasons spin
Themselves into ordained patterns
And there is a time when giving is done,
When the bloom withers and new seeds must sleep,
Wrapping silence about love's dreamings,
Feeding hearts and healing up the ravages
Of spring storms and summer droughts.
Like Psyche, I listen, waiting,
As reeds whisper, leaves dance
And Pan begins to sing.

Riverbed
for Virginia Woolf

Read what you please
In the silt and wet stench
Of green algae sliming
Wide pools of unseeing eyes.

When the disturbance
Of foaming bubbles and thrashing currents
Calmed, reflected voices
Stir startled gaggles of transient geese
Wintering amid the black bogs of peat
And marshbugs skittered across shifting pane

Water pipes
                showering broken notes
Left behind
              for unborn babes
To seize upon,
                for dry quills
To drink,
         for strange hikers to find,
In shadows of nameless lighthouses

Guiding fallen seafarers
                  to false harbor.

Read what you will,
ripping off stubborn buttons and flimsy eyelets,
Shucking off flesh
Like a scratchy woolen jumper,
To fill pockets with smooth riverstones
For Heart's final fare.

When the water voices fall,
The river begins
Unseen.

April Twilight

Mother-of-pearl clouds
Frame sun's golden afterglow
Through the silhouetted pines.

Shining green tapestries
Dangle from the nets
Of oak branches.

The early evening is heavy
With the fragrance of lilacs
With crushed violets.

Stripped of all wonder,
I close my eyes, wait wordless.
Soft winds wash over my face.

Serenity works my dazzled heart,
Silent hands kneading,
Cauterizing, reshaping.

Steady rains erase me.
Storm shakes me. I am not finished,
Have scarcely budded.

Life is not through with me yet.
Love has only begun
To polish my throbbing bones.

I sit quietly. Forever is now.
Whippoorwills sing mourning doves to sleep.
Moonlight collects in the hollow between my breasts.

A dog coughs in the darkened fields.
I am a pillar of fire, a burning bush,
The roses growing in the coming night.

December Snowfall

I am as cool, dispassionate as the snowflakes
Which shatter against the windowpanes, collect
About tree stumps, on the north steps,
Under the eave's drip. I am so cold now
Nothing touches me but light.
I watch the snow flurry in clouds and sheets
And I think of you, staring out
Into the cold dark between the bars on your window.
I reach out in the night to touch you.
Your spirit winces, shying aside.
You have walled me off, shut me out.
I count the snowflakes, taste them with my tongue.
I am all I have and hold: a dying Mother,
One mongrel hound, three cats and the full flower
Of my sleeping self. I have all I need to live. I survive, now.
Some say survival is resurrection undisguised.
Perhaps they speak truth. I know only I am alone, wrapped in swirls
Of flying snowflakes, barefooted, and it is not a bitter cold,
Only another dark season to winter, to weather.
How heavy these long nights must weigh upon your groping grow-
    ing heart!
You have such great distances to bridge, so many darks to mine,
So many spaces to close, fill out. I tremble — not from the cold
But love's bite. The snow is gentle to me, when you are not.
Snow does not pretend. Winter's kisses are strong.
They sting my teeth and tongue, yet I love their honesty.
I look out over the snow banking, gathering in drifts,
Remember the chill of your reluctant mouth
And brush ice splinters, frostfire from my lips.
I can do nothing more, now. I listen to the pellets of sleet,
Turn out the lights, wrap the thick quilts about my breasts
And dive down into green dreams.

Minor Oversight

I probably should have told you
I am a little bit
Of a witch, too

Nothing bad

Only small things:
I talk to the wind
And listen to the leaves
Murmuring in their verdant dreams.

I follow butterflies
Anywhere
Testing my own wings.

Cats and I can talk
Nonverbally, in purring rumbles
And coughs half-snarled.

I weave my dreams
Into the running threads
Of reality.

It is not enough to dream;
Hearts must also dare.

I work love charms
Under each new moon

And wake each morning
Bedded in the warm arms of sun.

I walk the woods and fields barefooted
Touch earth's naked power.
The thirst for new life
Drives me.
              Loving is hard work.

I am woman enough
To stand alone when I must,
To sing when I would rather weep,
To rise up like currents and tides,
To kneel when I could lose myself in antic dance,
To build rather than tear down,
To meet life with open arms
Cherish the sweet, accept the bitter cups
And go on, life being a song, a hymn of light.

If that is a witch,
I am it.

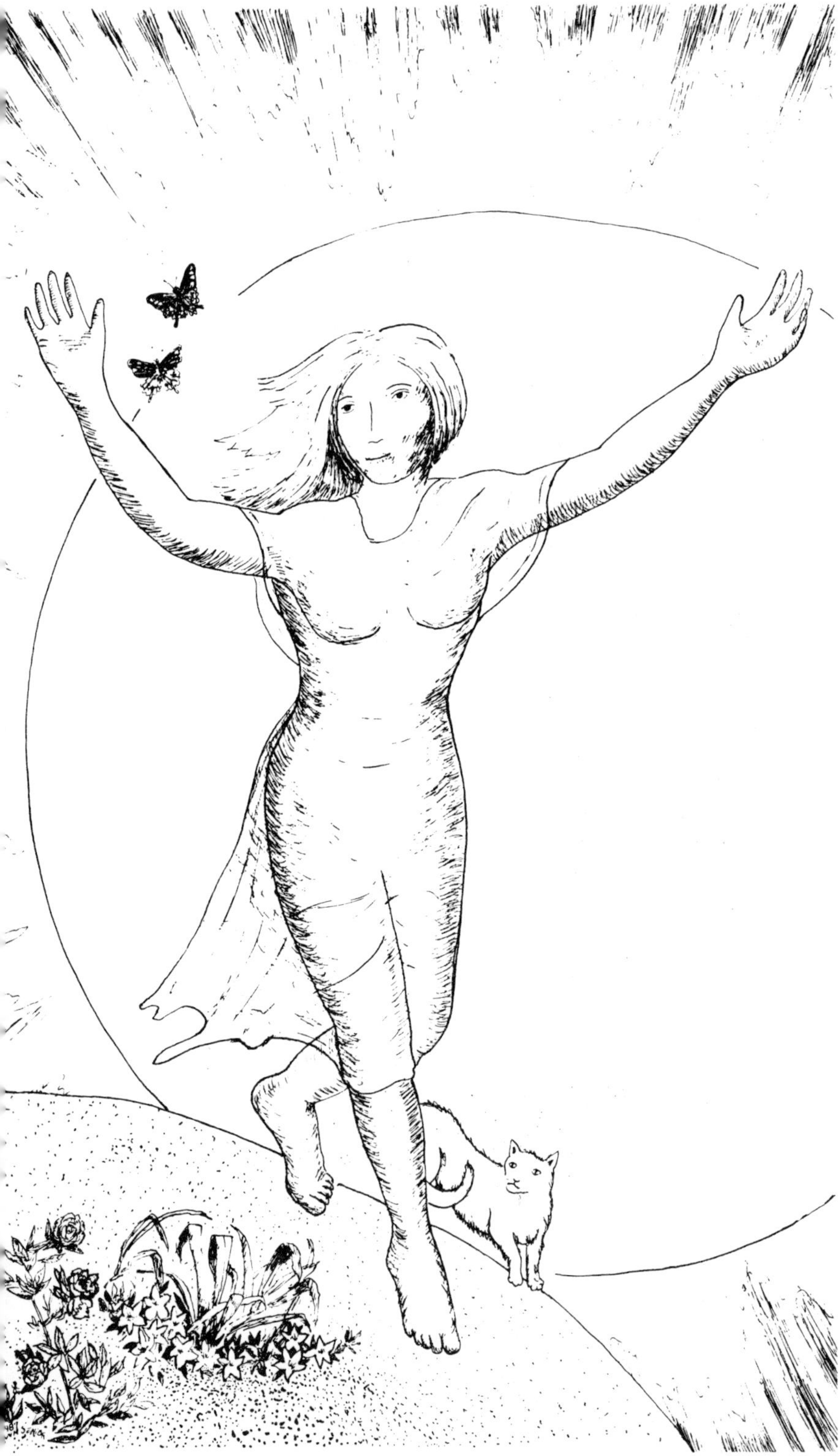

Love Potion

"I will show you a love potion without drug or herb or any witch's spell: if you wish to be loved, love." —Seneca

(for Mary, my dear friend, my sister)

And what magic more
Do we need than this, O beloved Sister?
What more than the flowers
Of our quickening hearts?
All cats are skinned the same way:
We range the forests of man's night
Under the cool harvest moon's sharp fires.
We go on our hands and our feet.
We change our spots, we disguise our tracks,
But we are always found out
By love's eyes burning in ebony midnight.
Use any charms you need,
O sister, I say unto you
Those who dare to love,
daily living out love in life,
are the lords of the morning,
are the true ladies of the night.
We bless ourselves,
Enriching hearts wherever we fly
Or fall.

Waters
for Jimmy Two-Rivers Stone

There is great magic
In the waters, the cool shaded springs
Surrounded by willow oaks, the gurgling trickle
Of small snaking creeks, the open thunder
Of roaring rivers, the bellowing laughter
Of the sea.
                Death and life lie dreamless
In the hidden deeps. There are other worlds
We snatch with peripheral vision
And sidelong glances; there are other voices
Murmuring and crashing upon the gray rocks
Which gape with naked jags of teeth.
There is a celestial music
Which paralyzes flesh, stops human hearts.

There is a clamorous might
Which leaps for life like bream splashing
In the sun-drenched shallows.
There are mirrors for the moon.
There are doors no key can touch
Or dispair lock away.

The waters bring life
And the waters bear death
And we are cleansed to the shivering bone.

Still the singing waters
Wash over our days in floods and storming tides

And what is meant to last
Will survive
Healing all.

Talking To Toci

When the first moon of this sudden savage spring
Kisses closed the eyes of midnight,
I will go with the wind
To my Grandmother's house in the woods.

Goodness haunts my heart.
She demands just reckonings.

"Set your sins before me,"
She invites. "Number them all.
I pick every bone clean."

"Life is more than lovings,"
She says, rocking by the hearth,
"Than being willing
To die or kill."

I sort out baskets of herbs,
Wash her feet. Clip her toenails,
Pour catnip tea. She teaches me
To eat my dead.

"Creation is yours,
Your heart is your own. You are never so wise
As when you think you are not,"
She croons, cradling my face
Between her wizened hands, "You jade,
Little moonstone, you wandering star."

Baby owls and tree frogs watch
As she casts lots with outgrown hearts,
With the broken jawbones of forgotten lovers.

"To live for another
Is a poor gift," she repeats
As she unbraids my hair.

Crickets sing <u>Toci Toci</u>
Until morning finds me
Shining alone.

Toci: "Our Grandmother", also known as Tlazolteotl, the Filth-Eater, Aztec fertility goddess who heard confessions and absolved mortal sins, but only once in each individual's lifetime.

The Byron Woman
for Mary Snotherly

The Byron woman is a composite,
Collage of diamond chips, a rare breed.
I am one of these.

She is bawdy, spring sweet and wind wild,
Magnificent beast of a Marianna Segati,
The elusive larkspur's first bloom,
Withering imperceptive, haunting foresaken rooms,
Mary Chaworth's specialty.
I am one of those.

The Byron woman is a walking contradiction,
A warped puzzle with catacornered missing pieces,
A starling soaring over Ravenna, Guiccioli proud,
Theresa in her riding habit of sky's brazen blue;
A frightened woodchuck scurrying through dry underbrush
Past midnight below Villa Diodati, watching
As Claire bolts, losing a satin shoe.
I have been there, too.

The Byron woman is contagious, a carrier of heat:
Squirrels gnawing at broken phials of paint,
Waltzing spaniels, moon-mad monkey
Plying frenzied ink, a wounded bitch
Lunging for naked throats, a pride of unmeek Lambs.
I qualify. Exceedingly.

The Byron woman is a natural disaster,
Spewing volcanoes, whirlwinds invited in,
Riptides, dolphins singing to tiger sharks
In murky waters black with boiling blood,
Marriages made in limbo going down and down.
I shun the formal name.

The Byron woman will not be domesticated,
Stays a goose with quiversful of virgin quills

Who fixes upon the now and never how,
Viewing the half depleted granary yet half full.
I know her better than any book.

The Byron woman can be underestimated
But seldom mistook. The Byron woman is August-
a buttress, a china wall, pussycat with dew claws,
Swordpricks dripping *octava rimas,* a witch with artless life.
I store up stanzas much as you.

The Byron woman lies down in love or not at all.
She flows like water's face, laughing scorn to death,
Owning no shame or loyalty other than destiny's next day.
She weathers well, knows love's way by heart,
Wearing heaven's hell with a careless grace.

We have spoken, face to face.

Missing In Action

Nefertiti, Queen of the Two Egypts,
Amarno's mother, Bride of the Sun,
Now less than a double handful of dust
Trickling through the scarab's eye socket,
More, perhaps, than a baby camel's bones
Picked to a gleaming precision
Under the desert's waning half moon,
Was only a woman, no more or better,
No worse or less, little different than you or me.
She and her history lie buried with her dreams,
Lost midpoint between Memphis and Thebes.
Her legend steeps, sprouts, taking root.
A fig tree uprears in my back yard
To reign regally in undisputed sway.
I remember Nerfertiti when the rising nightwinds
Rub their arching backs against the newly budded branches
And wonder if she, in turn, remembers me.

Quena*

I am a keepsake,
A snapped wishbone,
Lost music.

Through me pass symphonies
Of vanished light.

I am dark fires,
Smoldering memories of blood roses
And golden birds startled to premature flight.

**I am that forgotten hymn of smoky chambers
And flint knives brandished by hands of paradise.**

I swell, fill myself with holy air,
Spill lilting notes of silver litany
In the weeping moon's thin wake.

Quena is me,
Once loved,
Now singing bones.

---

* There is an instrument called the quena, made of human bones. It owes its origin to the worship of an Indian for his mistress. When she died, he made a flute out of her bones."
—Anais Nin

Whatever Shall Become Of Us?

The same as before: time will go on,
Suns rise and moons set. And we will go on
And life continue, the meaningless tedium
Of trying to survive, the daily crucifixions,
Nine to five, often overtime, petty squabbles
And backbitings . . . .

And so we limp along; blundering from disaster
To calamity, to rise up, shake ourselves like dogs
Scrambling out of a pond, to lurch on again,
Measuring ourselves, all those we love,
By the misunderstandings and many failings,
Keeping careful inventory
Of all the shattered dreams
Which flesh out our secret skies

Like clouds of peach and pear petals
In early April raining down, flailing
Against our greedy hands
In drunken gusts and sudden swirls.

And we dig in, bite down like turtles
Until it thunders, maintain, holding on, keep on
Loving, living, lying, laughing, cheating, sharing, dying
   Through the potholes and the hidden fog pockets,
    The scattered patches of dogwood blooms and unexpected sun-
      shine,
    The hidden pastures of gladness rediscovered, reclaimed . . .

And so we go on
   Never knowing   never caring   never bothering to puzzle out why
   It is enough   this sweet knowing   only how there is still something
    More   something alive   in our blood   our bones   our dreams
Never knowing where or when
   Only that there still is wildfire steeping   a small secret flame
   Within our homeless hearts   which is alive   which is us
   Which feeds   goads   drives us   even blind, broken, hopeless

Still that small flicker   something always trying
Drying, feeling, flying, falling, failing always dying failing only
To shoot up through us again   and again   and again we reach out
For new stars, broader braver skies, more moons   still hungry

Always hungering still living, laughing, loving, reaching, failing, dying

Forever rejoicing in the first dance
The festival   this Southern hoe-down   unending celebration
Of us — you and me — this sweetest mystery
Of being human, part-star, half dirt,
This only, this holy gift
Of being alive still

To love, love, love.

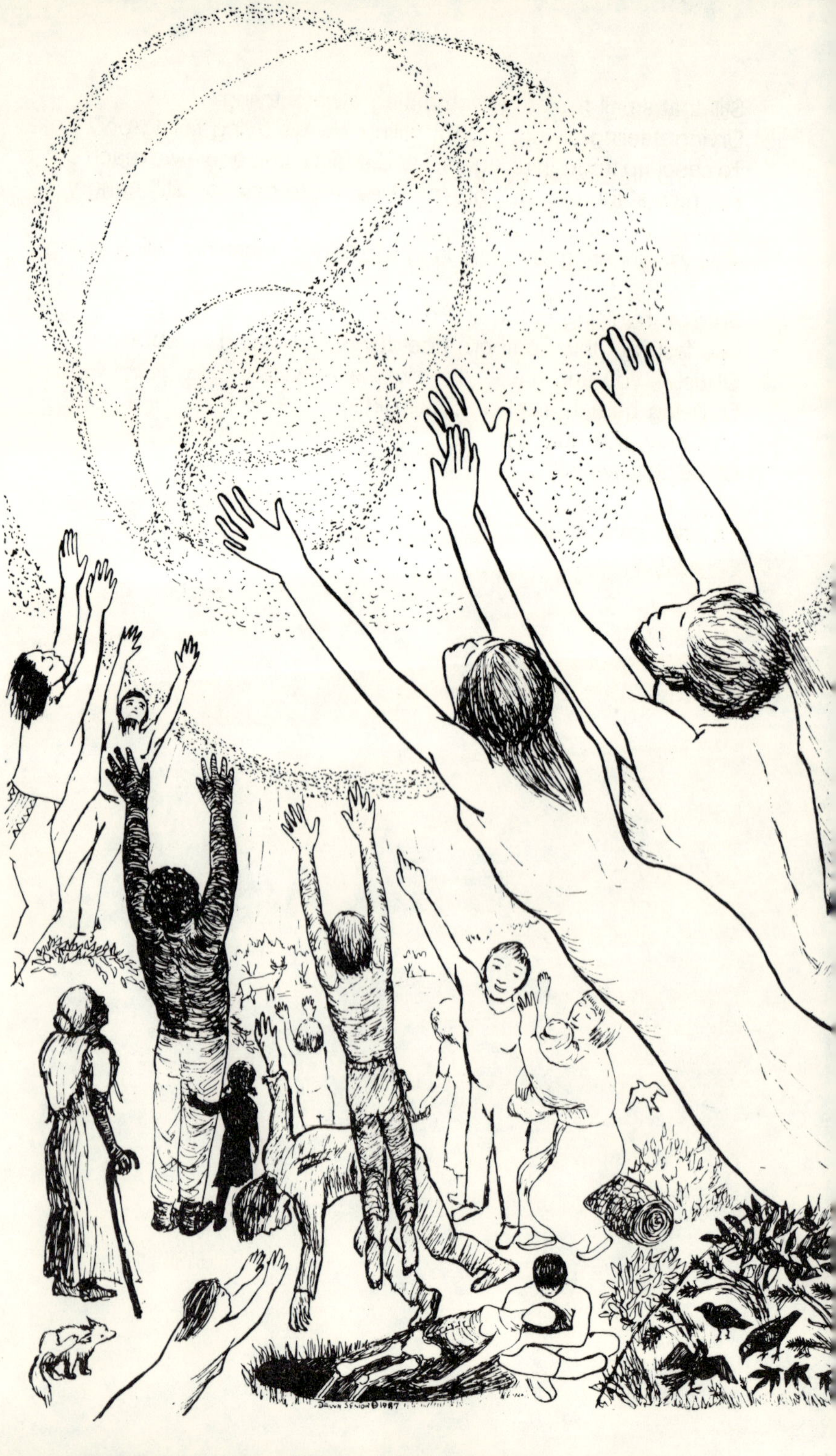
DAWN SENIOR © 1987

Divorce

The Dakota braves did it
In their white doeskin vests,
With four drummers stationed
Around the leaping campfires.
They braided hawk feathers
In their hair, dancing, singing,
Praising, shouting, performing
The Ceremony of Throwing
The Wife Away.

Sorrow sang from the south.
Moon hid in the west.
Celebration called from the east.
Death waited in the north.

Woman closed
Like a magnolia's pale petals
Dropped upon the bare ground.

The Wife had two choices
At the ritual's close:
To publicly accept
Being outcast;
Or quietly to hang herself
In the grove of willow oaks
At the water's edge.

That is why the stream is called
Hanging Woman Creek today.
Brevity being also the heart of despair,
"Divorce" is all we need to say.

Casting Of The Stones
(a grieving/mourning rite)
For Kenneth

"I have tasted of the sacred mushrooms
And my soul screams: <u>If only we lived forever,
If only we never had to die!</u>"

                                 From the Nahuatl

Following the death of an exceptionally valorous warrior,
Indian women would smear soot on their cheeks,
Rub dirt in their hair, walk out into the desert wilderness,
Collect a mound of rocks, then throw the stones
As far as grief could reach
And curse.

          I am throwing stones now,
Over the far mountains, behind the sun,
Raining on the moon.

               I swear at myself,
The things I should have told you and didn't,
At being powerless to free you, from life's many prisons;
At living too long and loving too late.

I aim jagged clumps of sharp quartz
At the faces of false friends, at opportunists
Who betrayed your trust; at hypocritical jackals.
I curse them all, by the moon, by my bones.
Nothing ever begun by them will end well.
All their greed will come to pass
And they will curse themselves. Nothing
Will grow or prosper which touches their hands.

I rail against time, human **imperfections,**
Against capricious chance, against a world
Without you.
             Sorrow is a granite slab
I hug against my dead heart. The only remedy
Is to bear it.

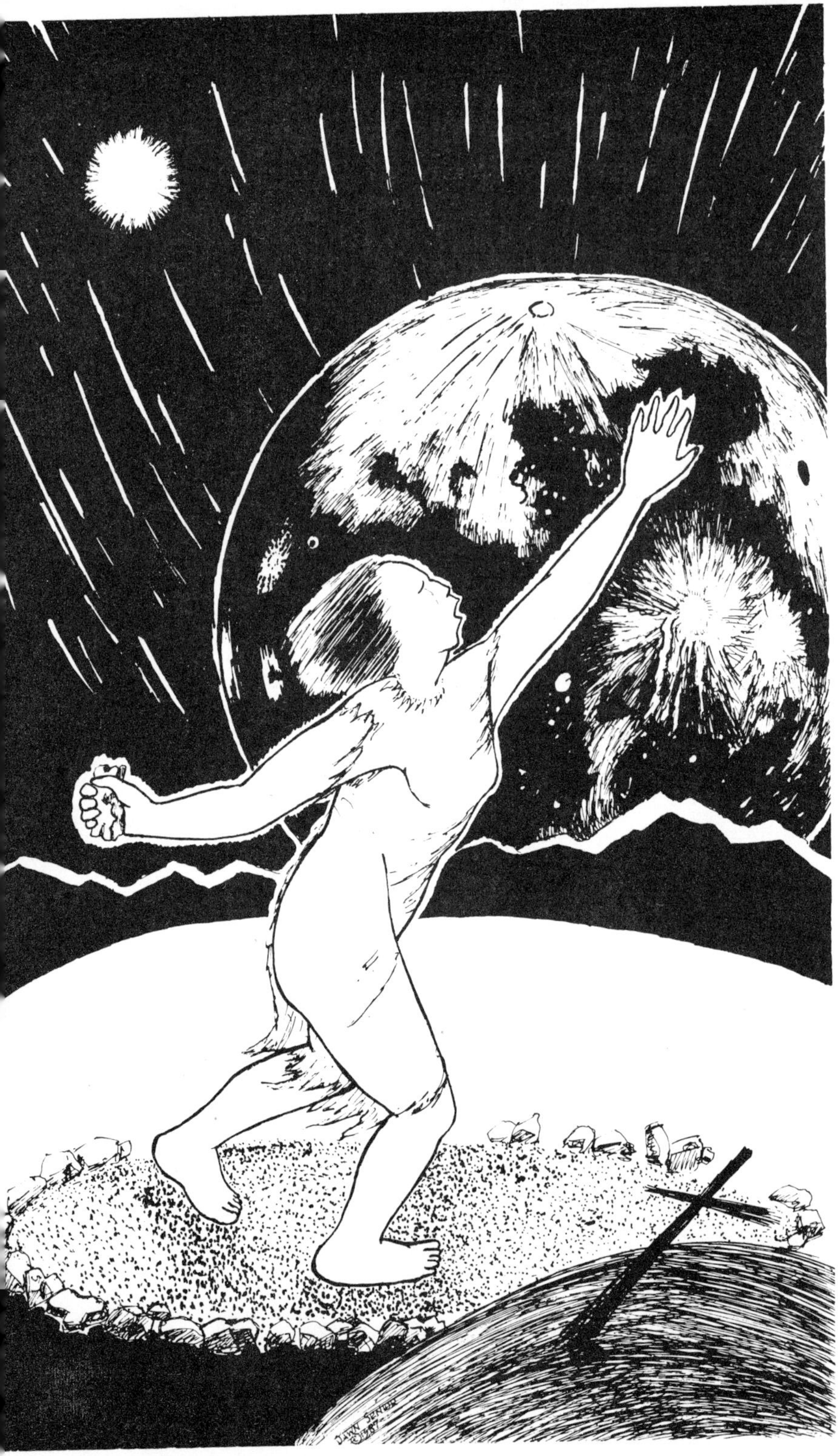

Lunar Dispatch I

You will never know all of me, Man.
I can be anyone, anything, any heart I please.
And I choose many: sometimes the little girl
With gold-spun angel hair and flesh pale as moonlight
Tugging excitedly at your open hand, the next minute
I am the old moon, wrinkled as a frost-sprinkled apple,
Dry and shriveled from want of harvest; and the next, a memory.
I do not try to hide myself or my seasons from you.
There is no need: you will never unriddle me,
Never seize the full mystery I am. My soul is unending.
I will always paint you new skies.
I shall always be changing, changing, growing inside,
The better to unveil more of life's gardens
Before your disbelieving eyes.
You will hate me as often as you love me
For I am knitted into your bones. I am the blood
To your veins, the pattern for your skin, air to your lungs.
I am the loom for your dreams, I am the mirror
where you meet love staring back and you will never know all
Of me, will never uproot my thirst for stars.

Lunar Dispatch II

Because I cannot come to you tonight
I will dispatch the moon
To keep watch, cradling your dreams
In her warm golden arms.

Because I cannot kiss your cheek
I will send the wind
To tease the tangled ringlets
And waves of your hair.

Because I cannot kiss you awake
In the drowsy morning
I ask the larks to linger close
So you might catch their trilling greetings.

Because I love you
The more I come to know you,
I fit you together like a thousand-piece jigsaw puzzle,
A rough edge here, a meaningless fragment there,
Catching my breath when the pieces fall
Into their preordained places,
Fragments fitting together into one shining whole.

Because I know you so little,
And want to love you more,
Deeper, stronger, more fiercely singing
Than ever I have loved before;
Because you draw out brave life in me
Like a compass returning to the North Star
Unerringly, over and over and over again,

I will spin you no shining webs
Of rainbow hues, tempt you with no fairy tales,
No happily-everafters or I dos and don'ts.
I will only bring you all I am,

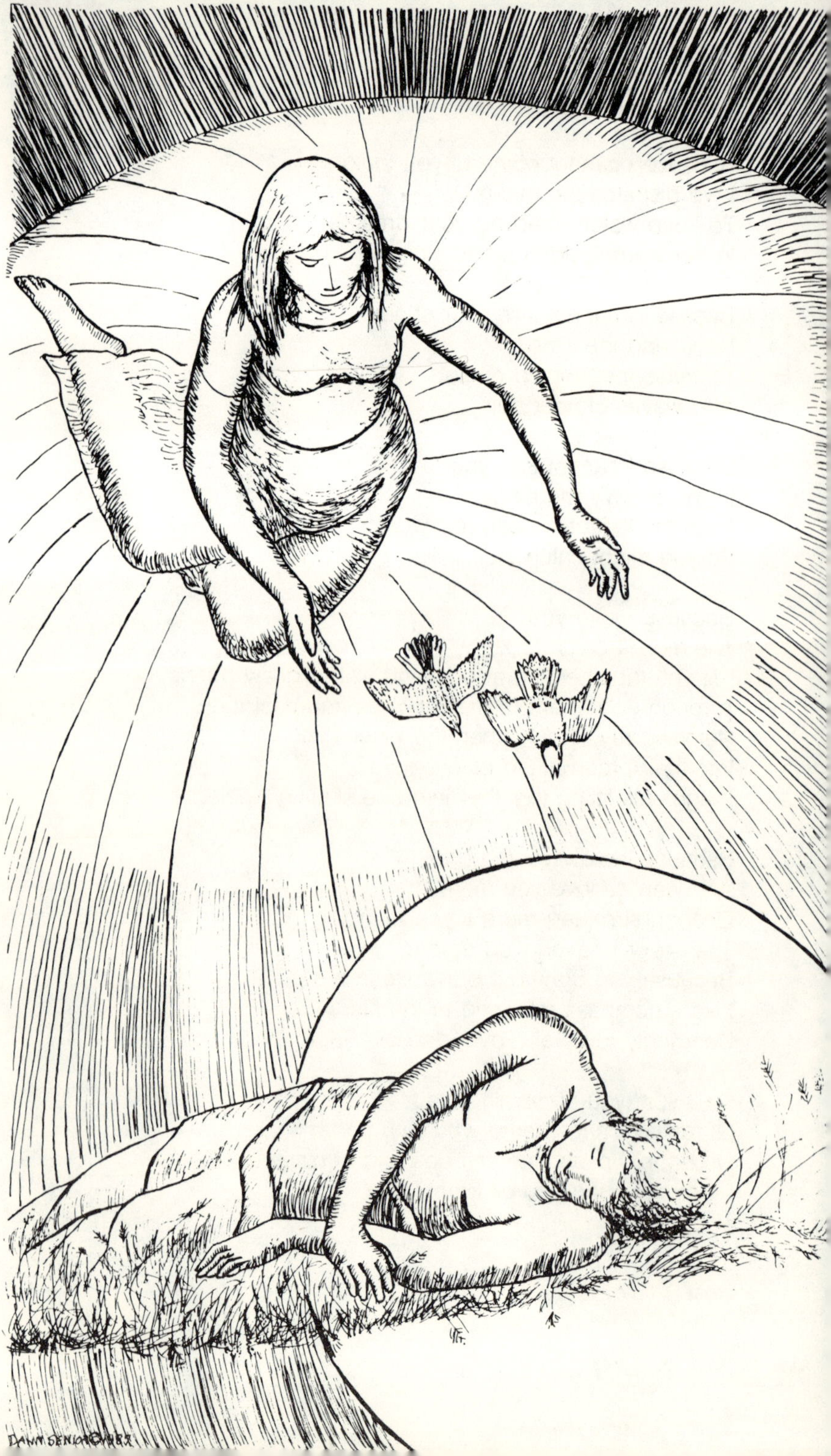

Lunar Dispatch III

I am leaving you now
Dying leaf by drowsy petal
While the last defiant roses dissolve
With summer, vanish inside love's lost dream.

I shake loving off. I wiggle, squirm, shed love,
Another seashell or dead snakeskin,
Outgrown, empty, useless.
My new scales gleam:
Emeralds, jaspers, jade.

I gather up love's broken cups,
Sift the wreckage, rake heaped ashes,
Stamp out the final stubborn embers
With dancing naked feet.

I break loving's crutch over my knee,
Smear soot on my forehead, my cheeks.
My spirit spins away from you
Another homeless ghost.

I burn your letters, study pictures
In the leaping flames, squint through coiling wisps
Of stinging smoke while the fire feeds.
Your words twist, curl, crawling
Like copperheads off the charring pages.

Death and fire, they cleanse, purify.

I am learning to be one alone.
In the shadow of man, things get lost,
Confused, stagnant, dry-rot.

I do not hide my light: I cast my own shadow now.
I have broken loving's last shackles,
Walk away rejoicing, whole, renewed, intact.

I wall off my heart: post Barbary leopards
At the foot of my bed to guard my dreams.
Obsidian butterflies sail by
On whispering clouds of unruly wings.

I am diamond hard, a tombstone in your hands.
I am safe. I am free. The dark mountains invite.
I wrap night about me. Wind opens its arms
To welcome me home.

Life on the moon is easy, sweet:
There are no men here.

Lunar Dispatch IV

I want to be like the moon

Mateless   matchless   shining alone

I want to be the winds
Forever rushing   searching
Sometimes laughing over the summer meadows
Burning with the wild daisies' rich gold
Whispering through the dancing pines
Howling across the brooding deserts
Weeping in the rainy nights

I want to be whole
Self-sufficient
By myself

I will feed the roaring tides
Of my hungry heart
With my own hands
I will nurse my private dreams
I will build sacred places palaces in air
Sweet and serene
Where I may enter in
At will

I will keep my self strong

I have so much to learn
So little time.
             If to let go
Means to forgive, then I forgive you
Every man who has walked through me
Like a door   wrapped me in cocoons
Of sugar-spun fairy tales   kept me weak
Ignorant   trained   constrained   chained
In your shadow   another echo   a mirror
Where in you might peer
And admire only yourself, your handiwork

I forgive you, each and all.
I will not have my heart my dreams my life
Haunted by hosts of lovers
Both buried and among the walking dead.

Lunar Dispatch V

With every love
There is a leaving
A letting go

Love cannot be caged

Love must be given
Like watering wandering dew
Measureless
Confident
Knowing the rivers of life
Can run underground
Some times   some seasons
But never dry

Say then love is another river

Where we can splash in the shallows
Like minnows and trout
Or float like turtles in the coves
Leaping with the otters and beavers
Through the choppy currents

Say love is the sea

There is no water on the moon
Yet I drink deep from dark's cool springs

To heal is to restore   renew

What shall our journey become
You ask me

Whatever we deem   desire   dream   build

Say love is an unending road

Where is there to go but now
Here   where
This gift of today
Where I find love wherever I cast my eyes
And I look everywhere

There is so much love in me
Sometimes I terrify myself

Say then love is air

I breathe you in
All my loves lovers friends kin
Those I know and cherish
Those I have yet to dream
Into being   I breathe you out
Slow   steady   sweet   I fill out
All my emptiness

Changing Moon
For Mary North

What can I tell you but what you too know?
The moon is always changing and man ever turning
Away like the tugging tides which pull us
Roll us like driftwood in the thundering breakers.
We splatter like the white frothing sea spume
Break over the gray rocks below the cliff's lip
And rise vanish in the blinding waves
Of sunlight, of starfire, of moonshine. We leave behind
Scattered gladness   sodden hanks of seaweed
Shark's teeth   empty conch shells too narrow
To nurture our growing groping homeless hearts.
We press medallions of coral   mother of pearl shards
Into the anonymous sands safe above the high tide's boundary
For new loves to wonder the waters which bore us
The ways we came, changing from child to girl
To woman; for more lovers to exclaim
The shining notes we drop from bone flutes
And the serene grace of windblown butterflies
Drifting in the treacherous riptides, how
Their lifeless wings are orange and black sails
Washed ashore like torn nets of lost grace.
What can I say or sing but the truth
All women hold, that inherent knowing
We are born alone, live and die alone,
That our flowers and our beds and our hearts are our own,
That there will be many moons and many men
To gladden our earth journeys, that love passes
Through us like wind through the dogwood blooms,
Like hummingbirds through the lattices of lilac clusters,
That we cannot touch love or arrest love's comings
And goings, turnings and leavings any more
Than we can ape Joshua and bid the sun be fixed still?
I say nothing, nothing. I can but dispatch
Love to comfort, to heal, embrace you from a great distance
And croon lullabyes while you sleep. I go to gather you
Wild roses from the open meadows. Was it birdsong,

Just then, or your echo rising with the north winds?
I know only there is always this solitary reckoning
And we cannot, must not turn away from the lost temple
Of our unflowered our untested selves;
We carry all the love we need
To feed life in the shrines of our own hearts.

The First Step

To follow after Sun,
That sacred golden bird
Which needs no earthly nest;
To hold to the lonely road
And learn to love homeless loneliness;
To look to the heart and ask nothing;
To accept the seasons the growing heart holds;
To walk the unending roads
Crowning lost mountains
Marked by abandoned temples;
To carry fire in naked hands,
To learn the fire's ways,
To be fire, a nameless flame,
To ever follow light
And welcome each pocket of dark,
Such is Woman's task
For earth.

To love the journey,
To become the road
Is the first step taken
Home.

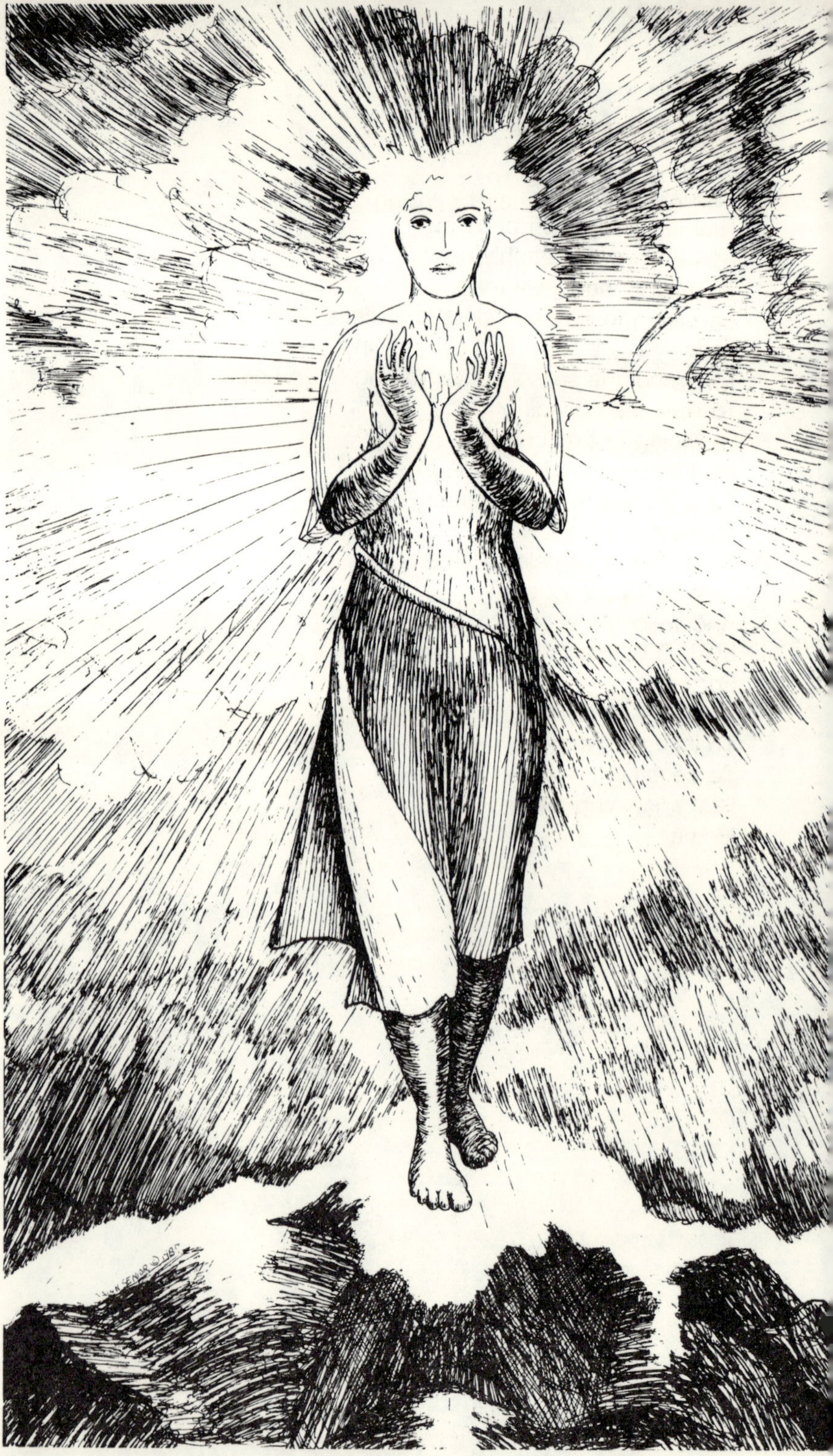

My Own Fires

I do not know whether this loving
Is worth love's final price.
I have lived so long making do
On half- and fractional loves,
Tablescraps and castaways.
I have been beggared so many times,
Broken like a twig, a matchstick,
Snapped, re-woven, quilted
And pieced back together
Like a shattered crystal vase
Or a Oaxacan wind chime
Savaged by the summer storm's sudden onslaught.
I am beginning to grow afraid
That only death is strong enough
To uproot the moon in me,
Slake this eternal need
For the love of a man,
Drown these rivers of fire, my blood.
I know only I want to stop
Drifting directionless
Like a pair of strange dice
Or a silver half dollar,
A maple leaf sailing in the wind.
I want to stop
Crucifying myself over and over,
Skip the instant replays, the dark brooding mountains,
The desert's naked heart
All open and empty.
I want to quit chasing ghosts
Of old lovers and dream lovers
With angelic eyes and Pan's sharp hooves.
I will make my own fires,
Carry love with me,
My turtleshell, a walnut husk for my home.
I shall leave nothing
But love in my wake.
I am making a start:
I will love myself first.

Amazon Patrol

Protected by moonlight's silvery mail,
They patrol the boundaries of dark
On horses black as midnight.
I would call out to them
But my tongue has lost their names.
I would run stumbling to their distant campfires
But my feet have forgotten the road home.
Even through the swirling pockets of fog
I can see their faces, a familiar curve
Of cheek, the firm jaw, the tender mouth,
The fierce burning eyes.
My Mother leads them.
They have come to strike off my chains.
I would go with them,
But for the man.
He says I have dreamed them,
An optical illusion,
The moonlight meshed with swift clouds
Reflecting off dead trees.
I poke behind imaginary shadows
To cultivate reality.
I cannot believe the music
They leave behind, he avows.
I nod agreement, watching how
Their long hair billows free
Like fields of ripening wheat,
Remembering how close they came,
How loud the slurping slosh
When they stopped for the horses
To drink from the culvert at the drive's mouth
And how long they called from the rose garden,
Wondering when I would leave the silent house
And naked as the night, rush
To fill my given space
In their swelling ranks.

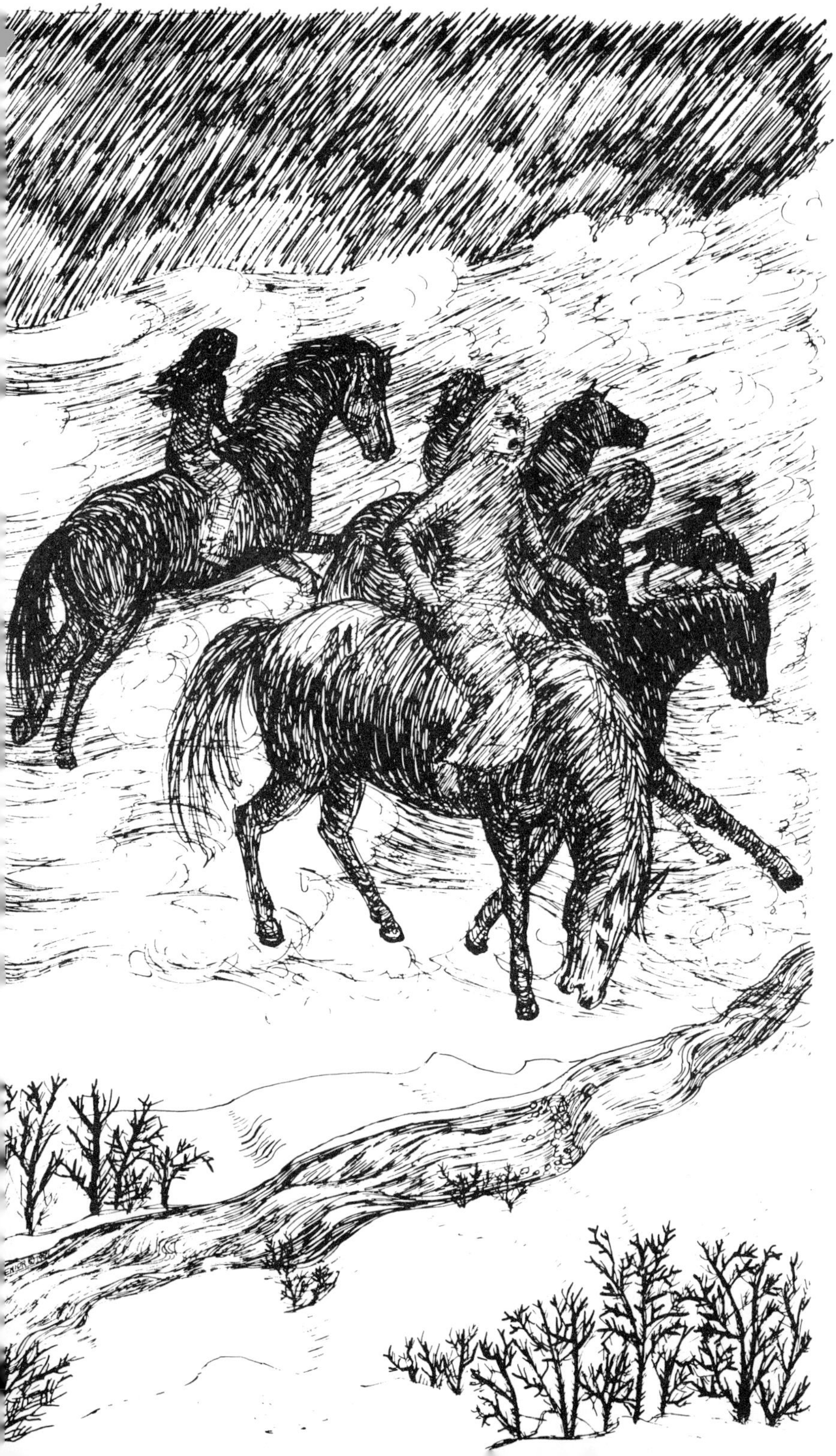

Memoirs of Snow White

The apple, as Eve's,
Perfect in symmetry,
Took my eye from the first.
Even the Hag's drooling laugh,
Prodding fingers upon my torso's flesh
Could not hold me back.
Why should I not feed,
I ask you, when stout tradition
Makes it mine?
Why spoil a prime story
Or alter a single line?
So with a good appetite
I ate it up, both peel
And core, seed and pulp.
But the charm played me false
And historians recount wrong.
Now I never sleep.
The Prince never comes.

Winter Over Estancia

Snowdrifts steady the leaning fences
And the narrow streets disappear.
Wind stirs the powdered window sills
And the thin fingers of light
Grope feebly through the closing darkness.

Billowing sheets of swirling snow
Are blown in shining whirlpools
About the swinging street lights.

The stark outlines of thick trees
Offer their mute guidance.

Straggling barbed wire is knitted
From post to post.

In the headlights' confused scrutiny
A coyote darts, adroitly bounding
From banked ice to the wide pasture's safety.
He looks back, once, over a shaggy shoulder,
Frost glittering along the sandstone fur,
Eyes flashing towards the far mountains
And is swallowed up
By the blinding whiteness.

Degrees Of Light

I am beginning

To see again, am learning
To read the subtle gradations
And degrees of light.

Sometimes there come snatches
Of translucent, random grace,
Spears of bright lucidity
Breaking dawning's black back.
Then there flame the golden arrows
Of new morning, noon's fully flowered white heat,
The afternoon's slow smoky haze
Gathering along the cedars and pines' treeline,
Amethyst, mother-of-pearl shimmering mists
Shot through with burning blue threads,
Then the silent radiance,
Silver, gold, sweet, wordless,
When the full moon finally comes home
To the waiting snowy fields.

At last I am beginning
To taste clarity.

I am not the center
Of the universe
Yet the center
Sleeps in me.

I am only a small
Nameless part of life
But without me
The world would be changed

Diminish   shrink   grow colder   more inhospitable
Less loving   darker   fruitless   more lonely.

To change the world
I must start with myself
For love, as charity,
Begins at home.

I remember Joan of Arc.
I remember the fires.
I account for my butterfly self
To the gods alone
And no man alive.

I remember Juana of the Cross,
Rustle my hair like her veils;
Like her I now know
Wisdom is nothing more
Than choosing life.

The Sunshine Girls
For Brenda

We have nearly forgotten how to speak.
Words bare claws, catch and rake
Our throats, erupt
In starts and stutters.
We sit quietly,
Exchange poems,
Swap horror tales,
Comparing escape routes.
We sort through the ruins,
Beg confirmation
Periodically,
"Was it like this
For you too?"
We have outdistanced
All our terrors,
Outgrown the golden cages,
Outlasted private deaths.
We are learning
To look down
Into the grave's open mouth,
Turn and walk away.
We are learning
The tongues of light.

A Birthing Song

Place the ripe cornears
By the doorsteps
For fruitful harvest.

Knife, cut my pains
As you will clip
The babe's cord,
Evenly, clean.

Mother,
Tell me again of that day
The sun died when I came
Thrust upon these turquoise waters
From my first bed beneath your heart.

Blood, I know you
For Woman's first ink.

I write the child's name
Across my straining belly.
I am thrashed   husked
Caught between grindstones.

Bones, bend. Remold.
Let the son of light pass.
Speed the daughter of forever on.

Child,
Even as you claim your crown
Between my legs
I grieve your coming
Into this bitter world
Which rips you from my womb
    Like a peeled orange,
    Liked a hided squirrel,
    Like a lost bird,
    Like a shivering song.

Little one, I rejoice
How we are both being born.
Hurry, O hurry to my impatient arms.

Squaw Winter
For Kenneth

A woman's heart in winter
Is a vacant field
Overgrown with dried witchweed
And dead brambles
Where foxes run
And deer thread on cautious feet
Between silent trees.
My ears strain
For the lost music of your voice
But only the wind speaks.
My eyes starve
For your shadow.
Nothing moves
But the hawk dancing
Along the south horizon.
My hands ache
To cradle your face
But I touch only air.
Now you are everywhere,
Both here and there,
Then and now.
                    Balancing
On the edge of time,
Your spirit grows stronger
As your flesh fails.
Even as you are dying,
You are being reborn.
I have shared living and loving
With you and now it is only right
That I should share the dying too.
We are becoming One
With the morning stars and soft steady rains,
With the dreaming fields and sleeping seeds.
I regret nothing, nothing.
I am blessed beyond belief.
We are sky, moon, earth, wildfire, sea.

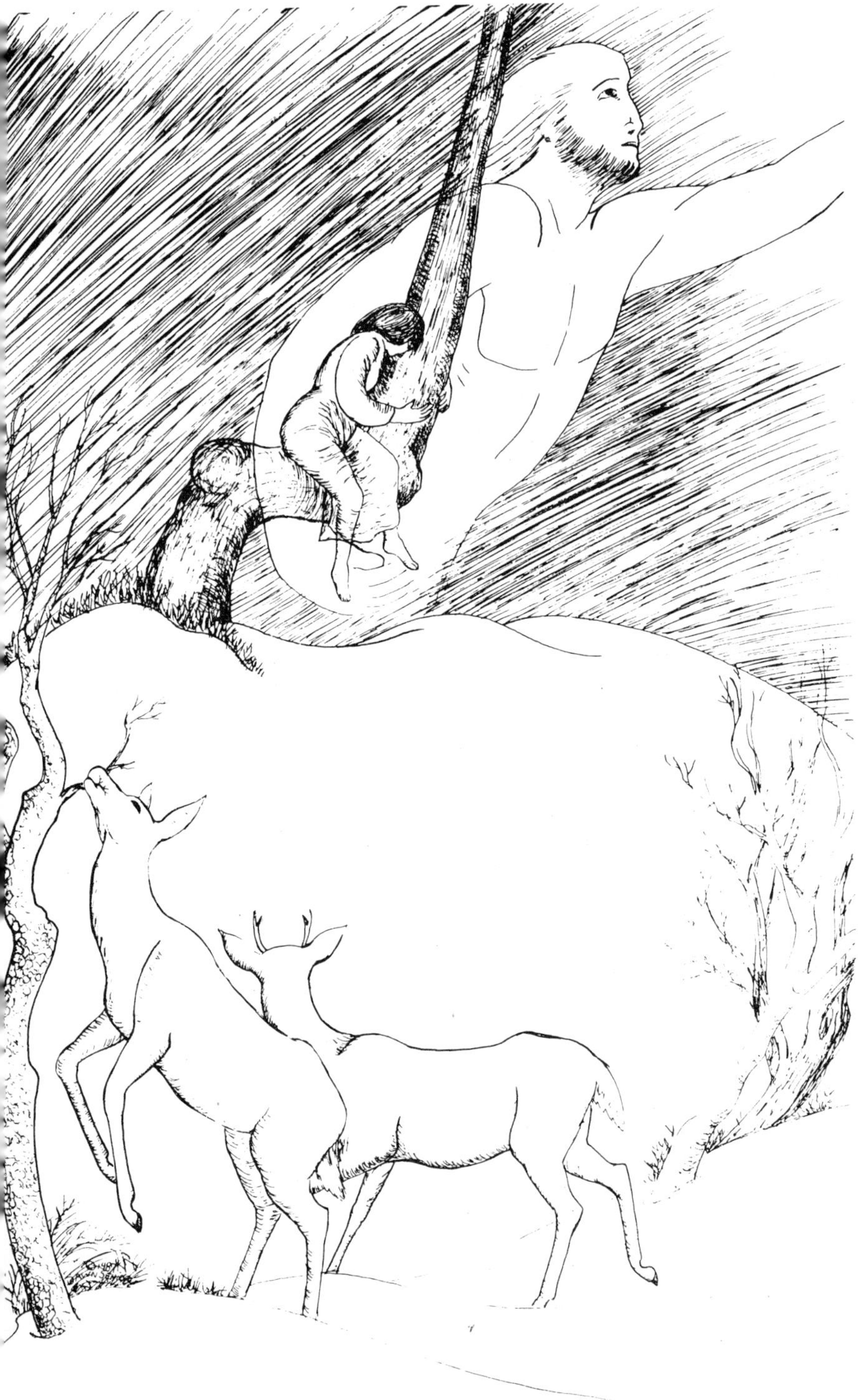

The Wise Woman
(A definition in the Nahuatl manner for Las Sabias Senoras Maria Sabina, Petrita Baca and Elaina Ramirez, and my Grandmother, Mae Magdalene Long-Whitfield)

The Wise Woman: she is a seeker, a singer, a seerer.
She does things, knows how to stop the world.
She is a star-shaker, she is a sky-walker.
She roots pussy willows and wild roses,
Plants and harvests. She dreams of light
Even in death's hard bed. The Wise Woman:
She is a heart teacher, a time weaver.
She comes and goes like the wind-swept moon.
She reads leaves, dries herbs, sings herself to sleep.
She is a campfollower, she is a soldier,
A holy warrior, fed on tender rue.
She heals the infirm, heartens the weak
With a sharp tongue and steaming verbena tea.
The Wise Woman: <u>dura mater</u>, a hard mother.
She keeps every counsel; her bed is her own.
She enriches life, loves herself first.
The Wise Woman: she questions, explores, sifts.
Her roaring spirit shines, a deathless flame.
She tames wild things, unchains tamed minds.
The Wise Woman: she works, wakes, takes all parts,
Completes, makes everything whole and new again.

14 Southern Cihuactuicatl

NOTE: In the course of translating Spanish and Nahuatl poetry, there surfaced references to "cihuacuicatl" (women-songs) and a smattering of fragmentary survivors of this Nahuatl form. These poems interpret how a contemporary woman-singer might sound in English. They were written as an exercise of both imagination and intuited knowledge, reaching for what Stephen Berg, in the preface to his Aztec translations, called "the voice with no skin".

This Is A Song From The Wise Woman: To Be Given To Budding Girls

O destiny's daughter
Why do you dance alone
Across dawn's floor,
Barely cracking Sky's door?

The good woman balances herself,
Needing no help to be free.

The good woman keeps a full heart
And an empty womb to shelter
Tomorrow's fields.

The good woman is born
When firefloods and burning rains
Baptize the puckered forehead
Of eternity.

I am a good woman.

I marry none but Sun.

These Are Field Songs
To Be Always Offered Up To Sky

1
The obsidian butterfly
Crosses Sun, filling up sky
And night comes home again.

2
Grandmother Owl says
Whistling women
And a gabbling turkey hen
Come to no good end.

3
The Lords-of-the-Morning
Smile down upon the young corn.
The Ladies-of-the-Evening
Rock the fields to sleep.

4
But I don't want to love you
The hummingbird cries.
But you do you do you
Root in my heart.

5
Following the deer
Over the far mountains,
Mother Moon shakes out
Her white skirt, covering earth.

This Is A Song Of Thanksgiving For Being Born Woman

How can the gods hold other than high hearts,
Beginning each day with a new sunrise?
How can they be but wise,
Devising creations to defy time?
How can I refuse to be all I am,
They holding hearts like mine
Balanced upon the catwalk of sky
Bridging Moon and Sun?
How can I not be like Them,
The Makers-of-All-Life?
How can I be other
Than the god's flower I am,
Woman?

This Is A Song Of The Lost Garden

Why did he go with me to the willows?
He walks with her in the roses now.

Why did he marry me in the moonlight
Only to vanish inside dawn's house?

The willows are bare now, stripped of song.
Roses are ringing their budded bells.

In yesterday's womb I float, stillborn,
Rocked by the laughter of dead wedding guests.

Why did he follow me to the willows?
Who waits weeping by the rosebeds now?

This Is A Song
For The Hummingbird-Warrior

You, who nest in jagged halves of walnut hulls;
You, who rest hovering, frozen between earth and sky;
You, who fly every garden, drinking the sweetest flowers dry;
You, who pierce Heart's guard with a whittled beak;
You, who never sing nor speak, who are always humming,
Hurrying from one sky to the next; You, who vanish
Into Sun's burnished eye, exploding dreaming stars;
You, whose heart is homeless, yet forever hungering,
You are a god, too. You come and go, like Them.

This Is A Field Song
To Be Offered Up When Drought Comes

Full moon,
Man three-quarter bloom.

Spreading roots,
Frail new corn shoots.

Love speaks.
Somewhere gods sleep.

Bitter, bitter, salted wine:
Woman heavy for harvest
In Man's growing time.

This Is A Song For The Authors-Of-Life

O You Makers-of-All-Being,
You sky lords and you womengods,
When I die please place me
In a sunflower seed
So I can shine for you again.

This Is A Song Of Quetzalpalalotl*

Wind, curry my wings.

Moon, give me your luminous sheen.

Sun, take me home
From what I find myself
To what I was
When you first spied me
Fleeing every garden where you were not.

O gods, I am changing, changing,
Even as I break black bread with dark.

O Father, I thank you
For giving me a heart never to be outgrown.

O Mother, I thank you
For your godchild, my brother Man.

Wind, come closer.
Wake my sleeping wings.

* Quetzalpalalotl: From the Nahuatl, meaning "...the Palace of the Butterfly-Bird..."

This Is A Song
Of The Dancing-Sad Man

Bones aching to howl the unspeakable,
To read those first sagas written only
Across the walls of that inmost solitary heart,
To see what slips the nets of eye's mortality,
To sing what no human tongue can tune,
You burn.
              Divine tasks call you out
And so you dance, dance, dance,
To the steady thunder of distant ghostdrums,
Measuring time by blood's rising tides,
In harmony with that silver silence so sweet
Any song would break Heart's charm,
Any syllable shatter the corridors of glass
Where you dance, weaving crystal sorrow
Into wind's symphonies, winning
Disillusioned gods back to Earth's narrow fold.

Dancing Man, Sad Man,
With grief tinting your obsidian eyes,
Be glad, O Man, be glad
The heart is a holy hunter,
Your heart strong enough
To string sorrow to your bow.

Dance, dance.
O be glad
Grace cannot be misplaced.

This Is The Song Of Xochitecatl*

I am the one who cares for flowers.
I am the one who feeds the seed.

I am the one who waters the fields of Man
With my rain of womanblood and womantears.

I am the one who cares for flowers.
I am the one who combs your wings.

I am the one sent to guard the hearth
And tend the Heart's first flame.

I am the one who swims through your dreams
Knitting up each wind-tattered sail.

I am the one who cools your flesh,
Warming your frostbitten bones.

I am the one who is fuel for holy fire.
I breathe upon your spirit's rising light.

I am the one who cares for flowers.
The gods made me to flower for Father Sun.

---

* Xochitecatl: From the Nahuatl, meaning ". . . one who cares for flowers . . .", said by Sahagun to be the name applied to women doomed as sacrifice to the divinities of the mountains.

This Is A Song Of Old Men

I love the old men beautiful
With their white wisps of shimmering hair
And their young hearts leaping
Like thrashing songbirds
Trapped in bone cages.

I love the old men surprised
Daily by sunrise and galloping dreams,
Enchanted by tenderness given gladly,
Stirred by resurrected roots
In winter's cold bed.

I love that wild tribe of old men, beautiful,
Big, wily and wise, rulers of the craggy kingdoms
Of their weathered selves.

I love them, those rare men
Time cannot touch but to polish
The brilliance of their one jewel,
Heart's jade, evergreen.

This Is A Song Of The Half-Woman

You
   gawky green girl
      trapped in Woman's gown.

You are a cornshuck doll.

When Man touches you,
You crumble

Fall apart between his hands.

This Is A Song Of The Half-Man

You
   balky brattish
      tripping over your own shoestrings.

You are an overgrown boy.

When Woman calls your blustery bluffs of love,
You cannot run
Fast enough.

This Is A Song of Loveless Need

Dogs of desire,
Why must you come
Tugging at my bedrobes,
Scratching against my bones,
When I am here
And my man there?

This Is A Moon-Song For My Brother Man

My heart   wildcat;
Your heat   sleeping songbird.

I stalk your steps, hunt the hunter.
I crouch, spring, smooth, curve into flesh.
You whirl, hurl up clouds
Of green feathers and golden plumes
Into curling coils.

You bury your fangs in my groves of furred snarls,
Shower the toustled grasslands
With the dew of diamonds
And winged need, striking
To find your first name
Carved into bloodstone
Across the marbled halls
Upon the singing rock
Behind the eternal altar of emptiness
Under the wilderness
Surrounding your missing mountain.

You are the fruit of the earth,
A simple man with a holy heart,
He-Who-Is-As-Close-To-My-Heart-
As-Morning-Is-To-Sun.

My heart   lost music,
Your heart   mute singer,

    Lord Love,
The-Giver-Of-The-Song.

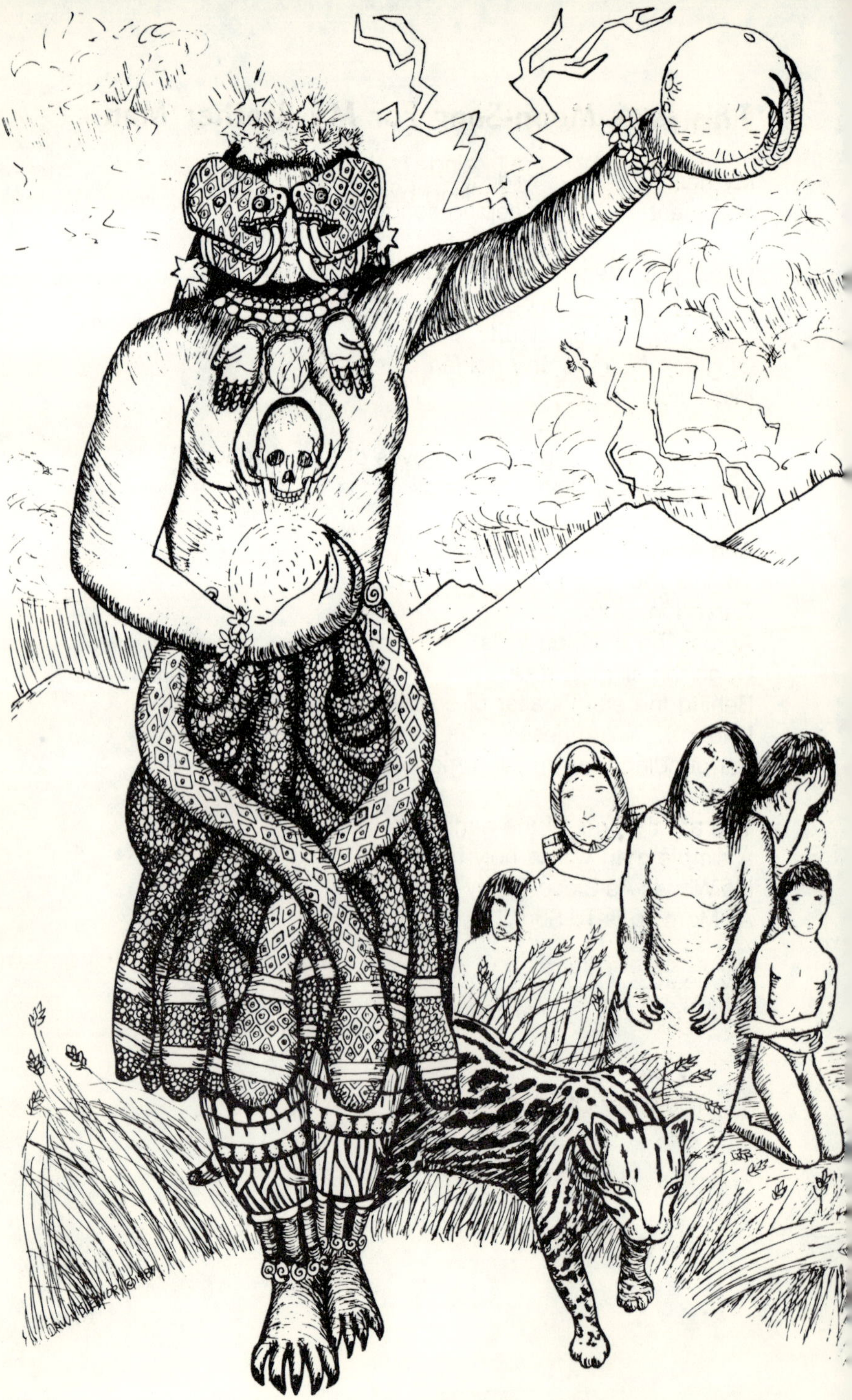

Hymn To Coatlicue

"I am the Mother of All-Being,
　The One who labored giving birth to the gods."

You are the Earth's Heart: we are the Earth's food.

She makes green grasses grow.
Coiling snakes are her petticoats.
She has five names: Mother Snake. Mother Eagle.
Mother Warrior. Mother of Hell. Mother Grass.

"My heart is turquoise, my womb, waiting jade."

You are the Ruler of the Night.

She gives sweet fruits to eat.
She lives close to the earth.
She flies with the Eagles.
She runs with the Ocelots.
She sleeps in earth's belly.
She cuts us down like wheat.

"I am the Giver of Life. I am the Giver of Death."

You are the butterfly with black wings.

White blossoms fill out her hands.
We string our hands and our hearts about her throat.
We weave black onyx with pale moonbeams for her
　　necklace.
Shall we ever O Mother behold your face?

She holds the Sun in her right hand.

"Moon sleeps in my left hand."

You are the Mother-Of-All-Living-Things.

She is the place of the red-flowering cactus.
She is the center, the cradle where we all began.
Bring her stag hearts. Bring her tiger claws.

"I am the Queen of the Heavens.
 I am the Mover of the Waters.
 I am the Thrower of Lightning.
 I am the Shaker, the Shaper of Mountains."

You are the Lady of Dawning.

Lost stars burn from her crown.
Snails measure her footsteps.
See how she wears stars in her hair!
Thirteen snails adorn her waist.

"I am the one who nourishes, makes whole.
 I am the one who heals, the eater of sins.
 I am the one who baptizes the dead."

You are Her: The One. The Gods' nest, our own.

She vanishes with the herds of hummingbirds.
She races over the mountains with the deer.
She dances on sunshine with the butterflies of song.
She rises with morning, bedding down with death each night.

"I wear Womanskin above my Heart."

You are a woman, too. Blessed be.

She bleeds, blessing us with the wine of her womb.
She rains the sun's fires down upon man.
Moon she sets aside for woman.

"None dare to speak my name."

You are The One ever over us all.
You are the Master of all the Heavens.
You are the Keeper of each Hell.

She is the Old Grandmother.
She delivers us into this cold bitter land.
She confesses us, absolving our sins.
She collects up our bones when breath is done.

"I am the Maker, the Mother."

You are the root of our human hearts.

Bring emerald stones, bring roasting corn-ears.
Bring nothing but your higher selves,
Your finest gifts and lasting songs back to Her.

"Forever is my home."

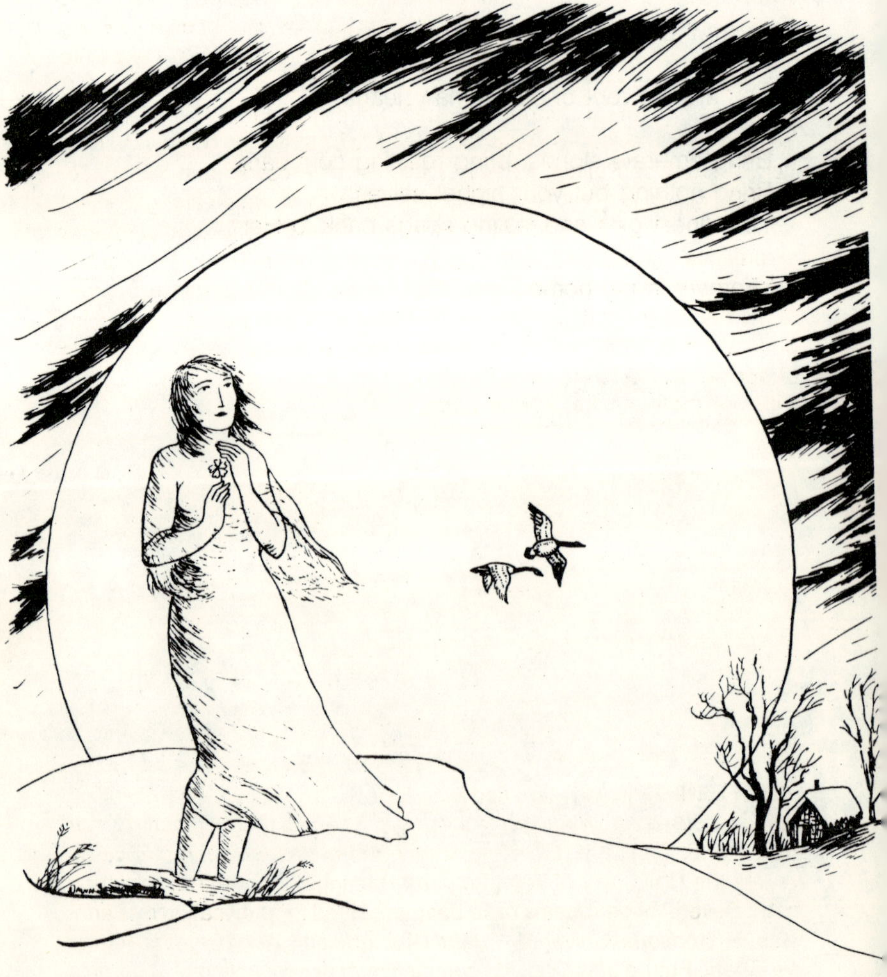

VIRGINIA LOVE LONG is an award-winning North Carolina author whose work has appeared in magazines, newspapers and literary journals in the United States, Mexico, South America and the United Kingdom. She was a N.C. Press Award recipient in 1969 and 1973 and her poems have been tapped for first place honors in competitions sponsored by the Poetry Council of N.C., the Greensboro Writers and the Sunbonnet Literary Festival. *After The Ifaluk And Other Poems* and *The Gallows Lord* were released under her byline of Virginia L. Rudder. Her translations of Spanish and Nahuatl literature appear under the name Mariposa. She was co-author with Rochelle Lynn Holt for *Letters of Human Nature*, nominated for a Pulitzer Prize in 1985 (Small Press Prose) and its sequel *Shared Journey: A Journal of Two Sister Souls*, which along with her popular *Upstream* were all Merging Media releases. She is an instructor of creative writing and active in the Poetry-in-the-Schools Program. Virginia is the mother of two sons, Michael and Shawn, and fostermother to a seven-year-old jaguar named Griswald. Her next volume, slated for publication in 1988, will be *All Roads Lead To Bushy Fork*, a collection of poems rooted in the rural Piedmont community where Virginia lives with her mother, Mrs. Myrtle Long.

DAWN SENIOR is Assistant and Art Editor of The Willow Bee Publishing House, a Saratoga, Wyoming small press. She was taught mostly by her father, W.F. Senior, a published author and professional artist. She attended the University of Wyoming and Hastings College, NE, majoring in art. Several of her poems have been accepted for publication by *Earthwise, International University Poetry Quarterly* and *Wyoming, the Hub of the Wheel.* Future plans include completion of her collection of children's stories and editing and completing her late father's unfinished book manuscripts. Dawn has recently been accepted for the Wyoming Artists-in-the-Schools program.

Other books by Virginia Love Long

UPSTREAM: A CELEBRATION

An elegiacal anthology celebrating the life of Kenneth Clyde Wagstaff, Jr. and a work of art by a poet who was his friend and love. $4

LETTERS OF HUMAN NATURE
(with Rochelle Lynn Holt)

The letter form is explored in poetic prose between two poets, one in the North and the other in the South to reveal how the moods of nature mirror those of the human who is also in constant flux here on earth. $3.95

SHARED JOURNEY: Journal of Two Sister Souls (with Rochelle Lynn Holt)

The sequel to Letters of Human Nature, two talented poets explore the human condition in beautiful language and with great insight. A moving experience for the reader. $3.95, or $7.50 for both

Please add $1.00 for postage and handling, mail orders to:

MERGING MEDIA
516 Gallows Hill Road
Cranford, NJ 07016